BEACH PARTY

PENGUIN BOOKS

UK | USA | Canada | Ireland | Australia
India | New Zealand | South Africa | China

Penguin Random House Australia

Penguin Random House Australia is part of the Penguin Random House group of companies whose addresses can be found at global.penguinrandomhouse.com.

First published by Penguin, an imprint of
Penguin Random House Australia Pty Ltd, in 2026

Mary Fowler is exclusively represented by Josh White at Always Human.

Illustrations by Cate James
Cover and internal design by Tony Palmer © Penguin Random House Australia Pty Ltd
Cover background images: diagonal pattern Alona Khadzhyoglo/stock.adobe.com;
wavy pattern Bijoy/stock.adobe.com
Author photograph by Simon Upton
Typeset by Midland Typesetters, Australia

Printed and bound in Australia by Griffin Press, an accredited
ISO AS/NZS 14001 Environmental Management Systems printer

NATIONAL LIBRARY OF AUSTRALIA
A catalogue record for this book is available from the National Library of Australia

MIX
Paper | Supporting responsible forestry
FSC www.fsc.org FSC® C018684

ISBN 978 1 76135 623 0 (Paperback)

We at Penguin Random House Australia acknowledge that Aboriginal and Torres Strait Islander peoples are the Traditional Custodians and the first storytellers of the lands on which we live and work. We honour Aboriginal and Torres Strait Islander peoples' continuous connection to Country, waters, skies and communities. We celebrate Aboriginal and Torres Strait Islander stories, traditions and living cultures; and we pay our respects to Elders past and present.

BEACH PARTY

Mary Fowler

With Jasmin McGaughey
Illustrations by Cate James

PENGUIN BOOKS

CHAPTER ONE

My name is Mary – Maz for short – and right now I am concentrating very hard. I don't want to make any mistakes!

I'm cutting some paper into the shape of the letter A to make a birthday card. The card is for

my friend, Anthony, who is turning seven today.

'Come on, Maz, we've got to get going,' Summer's dad says from the kitchen in their house.

'Almost done!' I tell him.

'A bit wonky, isn't it?' Summer says, beside me. She's my BFF and I slept over at her house last night so her dad could take us to the party. She's holding the present we got for Anthony.

'It's okay,' I say. 'Anthony won't mind. Plus, I'm pretty sure he's going to be distracted by his present.' It's sooo cool!

'True,' Summer agrees.

We bought Anthony a Frisbee Speeder 3000, which is a fancy frisbee that can fly through the air faster than birds and for longer than any other frisbee.

It's wrapped up in dark green wrapping paper – Anthony's favourite colour.

I finish signing our names on the card and then stick it to the present.

'Ready!' I tell them.

'Grab your hats, bags and sunscreen,' Summer's dad tells us as he jiggles his keys at the door. Summer's dad *hates* waiting for people.

My cow-shaped backpack (my most favourite backpack in the whole world) is by the front door,

so I put the present inside and make sure I have the things I need.

Because . . . Anthony's party is at the beach! I love going to the beach!

Summer's dad turns the radio up in the car on the way. All three of us love to sing as loudly as we can (even though Summer's voice gets scratchy and mine always breaks).

At the beach, it takes forever to find a park because there are so many people.

'Why don't they just go home?' Summer's dad grumbles.

'Because they want to swim in the ocean too,' I tell him.

He smiles at me. 'You're right. Maybe the parking fairies will be on our side.'

Summer and her dad think there are magical parking fairies that help them get car parks.

But I don't really believe in them. I don't think.

'Aha!' he says when he spots a park. 'See? The parking fairies are always looking out for us.'

We grab all the things we need out of the car and I put my backpack on.

'Look, Maz,' Summer says. 'Balloons.'

Green balloons are strung up on a table near a playground overlooking the beach. That's where I see my best friends!

SW
IM

'Maz! Summer!' they shout.

'Hi, everyone!' I wave, then Summer and I run over to them.

I can't wait for the party to start!

CHAPTER TWO

Before we're all allowed to go to the sand and water, Anthony's mum and dad point to a big bottle of sunscreen. We have to lather up on any skin that the sun might shine on.

'It smells funny,' Summer says.

Summer is a bit taller than me, with straight hair – though it is curling up today because she has it in pigtails. And right now she has a big handprint of sunscreen right on her forehead.

'You missed a spot,' I tell her and poke her head. When we're finished, the adults tell us to grab something and head down. I pick up a bag full of towels and walk with Summer and our friend Mitaru.

'The sand is hot!' Anthony yells from up the front of our group. 'Careful.'

'I'm keeping my shoes on,' I say. 'Just until we get closer to the water.'

'Me too!' Summer says.

The others leave their shoes on the grassy area next to the sand.

'Ouch!' says Kema.

'Ouch!' repeats Jazarah.

'Someone carry me!' says Mitaru.

'You're being dramatic,' says Anthony.

We all burst out laughing, and I'm glad I still have my shoes on.

The parents set up some umbrellas for shade and we throw towels down to sit on under them.

'What do you want to do first, Anthony?' I ask.

He thinks, tapping his finger to his chin. 'Let's make a pool.'

'A pool?' Kema asks. 'At the beach?'

'We could go for a swim in the saltwater!' Mitaru says, pointing to the waves splashing between the lifeguard flags.

'I want to build a pool in the sand and then fill it with ocean water,' Anthony tells us.

'We could dig a line from the water to the pool,' I suggest. 'So it fills itself up.'

Anthony grins at me. 'Exactly!'

We get to work. The pool takes lots and lots of digging.

After a while, Kema, Summer and Jazarah stay focused on the pool while Anthony and Mitaru begin working on a sandcastle next to it. A huge castle that will give anyone in the pool a cool view, Anthony says.

I decide to build a pool chair so I can stretch out my legs and relax by the pool. I gather up heaps of sand and pat it into a chair shape.

I am having the best time!

After a while, Kemi, Summer and Jazarah stay focused on the pool while Anthony and Miloni begin working on a sandcastle next to it. A huge castle that will give [illegible]

[illegible]

[illegible] the night away!

CHAPTER THREE

'Oh my gosh,' I say. 'It's gigantic!'

I'm looking at the sandcastle that Anthony and Mitaru are finishing now. It looks so good!

I pack the sand on the side of my chair to make it look like a pool lounge chair. I make the top steep so I can lean back and enjoy the view of the waves.

The pool we made is almost ready to be filled. Everything looks amazing!

The sandcastle comes up to my belly button and it's so cool! It's next to the pool where Kema and Jazarah are standing.

Summer brings a bucket of water from the ocean.

'Wow, Anthony. You two did such a good job. Look, there's a window!' Summer says.

I trudge through the sand to get a closer look. And Summer is right. On the tallest round tower, Anthony has made little window shapes with his shovel. On a smaller tower, Mitaru is placing shells around the top like beach decorations.

'I think you should build homes when you grow up,' I say.

Anthony grins at me. Sand is all over his face and in his hair. 'I think I want to be a professional sandcastle builder,' he says. 'People do that, right?'

Everybody shrugs, but I nod my head. 'Yeah, they build sandcastles as their art. You could be a sand artist!'

Anthony looks happy with that. 'Well, let's go get a drink and then have a swim.'

'We brought boogie boards!' Kema says.

'Aren't they called body boards?' Jazarah says.

Kema just shrugs.

We're about to head up the beach to where the parents are – when it happens.

The catastrophe.

BARK!

BARK!

My friends and I freeze then turn towards the sound.

'There!' Mitaru says, pointing.

I follow his finger and see a big, beautiful golden retriever sprinting along the beach with her tongue hanging out.

'She's so cute!' Jazarah says.

'That's Firework, my Aunty Shay's dog,' Anthony says. 'Look, Aunty Shay's running behind her.'

We see a tall woman racing to catch up with Firework.

'Firework is an interesting name,' Summer mutters. 'She's very pretty, though.'

'And she's coming this way,' Kema says slowly.

The dog *is* coming our way. Actually . . .

'She's heading towards the castle!' I shout.

But none of us are quick enough. All we can do is yell, 'NOOOOO!' all at once as Firework runs straight THROUGH the castle!

CHAPTER FOUR

The sandcastle tumbles and most of the sand falls into the hole we were making for the pool – filling it all up!

'Nooooo!' Anthony yells as he sinks to his knees and holds his head. 'My pool! My castle!

They're both ruined! What do we do now?'

Firework runs up to us and shakes her whole body. Sand flies everywhere and covers all of us. Firework doesn't seem to understand that she has upset Anthony. She sits in front of me with a big smile and her tongue hanging out of her mouth.

Anthony's Aunty Shay comes up to us, puffing. 'Sorry, kids. She got away from me.'

'Is it okay to pat her?' I ask.

'Sure,' Aunty Shay says.

I kneel on the sand in front of Firework.

'Hi there, girl,' I say.

The others start inspecting the damage Firework has done, so I figure I should comfort her so she doesn't feel too guilty.

I give her some scratches between her ears and she wags her tail really fast.

'It's okay, Firework,' I say. 'We know you didn't mean it.'

'Yeah,' Anthony says, giving Firework a scratch on the back.

'I'll take her up for some water,' Anthony's Aunty Shay says. She attaches a leash to Firework and leads her away.

'What should we do now, Maz?' he asks. 'I didn't want to get into the water until later, when it's nice and warm.'

'We could play tag?' I ask.

Anthony nods, but he doesn't seem very excited.

I feel bad because it's Anthony's birthday party and he should feel happy. It's his special day!

Then I have an idea.

'Anthony! How about you open the present Summer and I got you? We might be able to play a game with it.'

Anthony's whole body lifts up straighter and his eyes brighten. 'Oh?' he says.

'Yeah, come on. Hey, everyone!' I yell to the others. 'Come and see – Anthony is going to open one of his presents!'

Our friends hurry over to us, and we make our way back to the grown-ups. I get my cow backpack, and we settle down on the towels under one of the big umbrellas.

'Here you go,' I say, taking out the gift.

Giving people presents is so much fun! I love watching them try to figure out what it is and then get excited when they open it.

Anthony turns the present over in his lap and pulls off the card shaped like an A.

'Did you make this card, Maz?' he asks.

I nod excitedly and he whispers, 'Cool.'

'Well, come on,' Mitaru says.

'Open it!' Summer nudges Anthony.

Anthony tears the paper and then gasps.

'Oh, Maz,' he says with a huge smile, 'you and Summer got me a Frisbee Speeder 3000? This is the best!'

CHAPTER FIVE

Anthony passes the frisbee around and everyone turns it in their hands to look at it from every angle.

'Should we play?' Jazarah asks.

'Definitely,' Summer says. 'Do we play in teams?'

'We could play like it's football,' I suggest. 'We have two teams and we each try to throw it into the other team's goal. If it touches the ground, the other team gets it. Okay?'

'Perfect,' Anthony says, jumping to his feet. 'Let's do this!'

We split into two teams.

Team One: Anthony, Mitaru, Kema.

Team Two: Maz (that's me!), Summer, Jazarah.

We spread out on the harder sand near the water and build

SW
IM

small hills of sand to mark the goals. We make it a long field because a frisbee can be thrown really far – especially if it's the Frisbee Speeder 3000.

'Dad!' Summer yells when it's time to start. 'Could you please throw the frisbee to start our game?'

Her dad jogs over and is a little wobbly on the soft sand until he reaches the firm sand.

'You kids ready to compete?' he asks. 'You know, in my day, I was a pretty good frisbee player.'

Summer's dad throws the frisbee up, but this frisbee must be much more powerful than what he's used to. It flies up *high*. And he isn't watching! He just holds his hand out!

I try to warn him, but it's too late!

The frisbee bops Summer's dad on the head.

'Ouch.' He rubs his head and we all try not to laugh.

'Are you okay?' I ask, giggling.

He gives me a smile and keeps rubbing his head. 'Yeah, Maz, I'm okay. Might have to get some practice in.'

He picks up the frisbee and checks that we're all ready. 'On the count of three, I throw it, okay?'

'Okay!' we all shout.

I keep my knees bent and my hands out so I am balanced and ready to jump and run and throw and catch. Let's play frisbee!

He throws the frisbee in the middle of our group and we all run to it. The frisbee is *fast*. It zooms through the air and I step, leap and reach . . .

I catch the frisbee, which means my team has it first.

'Whoop!' I cheer and then look for someone to throw it to.

'Here, Maz!' Summer shouts. She is jumping up and waving her arms.

I hold the frisbee in two fingers, turn my whole body with it, and then spin and release. It soars above our heads.

'Whoa!' someone says.

Summer jumps and catches it with two hands.

The game has officially begun!

CHAPTER SIX

Playing frisbee on a sunny day can be hard, mostly because the sun gets in my eyes and the frisbee is so thin that it's hard to see.

Mitaru has the frisbee, but he's holding it like you'd hold a rugby ball. When he throws it, it cuts through the air straight up instead of horizontal like a plate.

'Whoops,' Mitaru says.

'It's still going pretty far,' I say as we all watch the frisbee.

Kema is standing in its path and jumps up, snatching it from the air.

'Good job, Kema!' I say.

I run so I'm further away from Kem and closer to the goal.

Anthony runs beside me. When Kema throws the frisbee, it'll be Anthony and me trying to catch it.

Anthony is taller than me, but

I'm very fast. So, I speed over the sand and turn and jump and I see that Kema has already tossed the frisbee.

I jump and catch it!

Before I can think too much and before Anthony can catch up, I twist my body around the frisbee and then spin and let it go free. The frisbee flies right between the hills of sand.

'Goal!' I shout, jumping up and down.

'You're so quick!' Anthony says, huffing and puffing.

I jog to grab the frisbee.

'Your team has it now,' I say.

'Thanks, Maz.'

The game moves quickly for a moment and we *all* start to get out of breath. Our running and jumping and even face planting in the sand (that was me) has made the sand soft, which means it's harder to run on.

'Maybe we should take a break and eat some lunch?' Anthony suggests.

'Good idea,' Summer says.

'One more toss!' Jazarah says, urging on Anthony.

'One more,' Anthony agrees with a big smile.

He has the frisbee and throws it with a grunt.

It soars high, whistling with speed!

'Oh no,' says Anthony.

'Oh nooo,' I echo when I realise what's wrong.

The frisbee flies over the shore and the small wave. It keeps flying and lands in the sea. Far away from us.

CHAPTER SEVEN

'How are we going to get that?' Jazarah asks.

'We're not allowed to swim outside the flags,' Anthony adds.

'Even if we could, that's way too far out,' Kema says.

'Maybe we could ask your mum, Summer?' I say. 'She's a great swimmer.'

Summer's mum once took us to the local pool. Summer and I played in the shallow kids' pool while a lifeguard watched over us. When we were done, we sat on the cement grandstands and watched Summer's mum do laps in the big Olympic-sized pool. She was such a smooth swimmer, she looked like she was gliding through the water. And she just kept on going and going.

'She is,' Summer agrees. 'But she didn't bring her swimmers. She said she didn't feel like swimming today.'

'I wish we had a boat,' Kema says. 'We could row out and get the frisbee.'

'We could make a boat?' Mitaru suggests. 'With boogie boards and floaties?'

'But imagine if it broke while we were way out there.' I point to where the frisbee is bobbing in the waves. 'That would not be fun.'

Anthony sighs and his shoulders slump.

Something brushes past me and I jump out of the way. It's Firework.

'What are you doing, girl?' I ask as she keeps running towards the water.

She hesitates as a small wave rolls towards her. And then she trots further into the sea.

'Firework is going to rescue the frisbee!' Summer says.

Firework starts swimming and I'm very glad the waves aren't too big today. She is doggy paddling.

SWIM

'Be careful, Firework!' Anthony calls.

She snatches the frisbee up in her jaws and slowly turns around until she is swimming back to us.

'You've got this, Firework!' Anthony shouts.

'Come on – go, Firework!' Mitaru adds.

'Go, Firework, go!' we all shout together. 'Go, Firework, go!'

Firework must hear us, because she swims faster and faster. The bright frisbee helps us keep watch over her.

And then, finally, she is in the shallows and can walk up to the sand.

'Good girl!' we all shout as we run up to her.

Firework looks tired, but also very pleased that she has so much attention from us. She drops the frisbee to let us cuddle her and scratch her wet fur.

Then she shimmies away from us and SHAKES.

The water on her coat sprays us and we giggle and squeal.

'Kids!' Anthony's mum shouts. 'Come grab some food!'

'Let's go, Firework,' I say. 'Maybe there's some food for you too.'

She runs by my side the whole way back.

CHAPTER EIGHT

The beach towels are covered in amazing-looking food. Here is what's on offer:

- Cut-up fruit (including mango, which is my favourite fruit ever).
- Tiny chocolate muffins.
- Party pies and sausage rolls.

- Scones with jam already inside.
- Carrot sticks with a delicious green dip.
- Fairy bread.

Anthony's Aunty Shay has a little station where we can make some fun drinks. Summer and I sit down with her first.

'All right, Maz and Summer. Choose which cup you'd like,' Aunty Shay says.

She has a box full of fancy cups. Summer and I both choose one with rainbow sparkles around the rim.

'Now dip it into this bowl of syrup,' Aunty Shay instructs, holding a bowl out to us. 'And then dip it into this bowl, it's full of popping candy!'

'Oooo,' Summer and I say.

The popping candy is bright pink and green. And it coats the rim of our cups.

'Now choose your drink.'

I choose a fizzy orange drink and Summer chooses a pink cordial.

'Take a sip,' Aunty Shay says.

Summer and I look at each other. We raise our glasses up and sip.

Pop!

Crackle!

Fizz!

'Those lollies are definitely popping in my mouth!' I say.

'Me too!' Summer says. She squishes her eyes closed but I think she likes the taste, because she goes back in for more.

* * *

'Ready to go swimming?' Summer's dad asks after we've rested for a bit.

'We are!' I say.

Some of the parents are coming swimming with us and others are lying down reading their books or even sleeping. In fact, I think I hear a snore coming from Kema's dad.

We put on more sunscreen and listen to the adults who tell us the rules.

- Stay together in the ocean.
- Don't go too far.
- Wear floaties if you're not a strong swimmer.
- Stay between the flags.

'Got it!' we say.

'Race you to the flags!' Anthony says. 'Ready . . . Set . . . Go!'

'Hey!' Mitaru shouts because Anthony doesn't wait for us to be ready. He zooms off as he says the word 'go'.

Mitaru darts off next and Jazarah does too and so does Kema. They catch up quickly.

'I can't be bothered to run,' I say to Summer. 'Let's walk slowly and see if we can find any cool shells.'

'Good idea!'

Firework follows next to Summer and me as we find shells with little holes in the centre. We save them to make necklaces with later and then we decide it's time to swim.

Firework sits at one of the red-and-yellow flags and watches as we make our way into the water.

'I think she's too tired to swim again,' Summer says with a laugh.

'I'm tired too,' I say as we wade deeper into the ocean. 'The water's really warm, but I don't think I'll swim for long.'

This is how I like to swim in the ocean:

- Dip and duck under the waves.
- Body surf the waves to carry me back into shore.
- Play mermaids and flip my tail in the water.
- Stand in the shallows and feel myself sink into the sand with each wave that comes and goes.

Eventually, Aunty Shay comes down and calls us back up from the water. 'Let's give Firework a quick wash and then it'll be time for cake,' she says.

Cake is the best part of any birthday!

CHAPTER NINE

The beach showers are up on the grassy area between the sand and the car park. Aunty Shay keeps Firework on a leash as we follow them up the beach.

'Someone needs to keep pressing the water button so

we can wash the sand off Firework. Kema, could you do that, please?'

'Sure!' Kema stands at the shower button, ready to press it.

'And someone needs to use this brush to get her tangles out.'

'Oh, can I do it, please?' Mitaru asks.

'Yep, here you go. Summer, Jazarah and Anthony – you three are in charge of soap. Keep Firework's coat lathered up, okay?'

'And what about me?' I ask.

Aunty Shay hands me a bag. 'You get to give Firework treats when she listens, all right?'

'Oh, thanks!' I say. This is so exciting!

Kema turns the shower on. At first, Firework doesn't want to get under the water, but Aunty Shay moves her gently.

Summer, Jazarah and Anthony squeeze some soap onto their hands and rub it into Firework's coat. The soap lathers up and covers their arms – all the way up to their elbows.

SWIM

Firework's tail wags and soap flies all over Summer.

'Ahhh!' Summer shouts, but she laughs too.

'Don't forget her belly,' Aunty Shay says.

Suddenly the water stops.

Firework uses the break to shake and now all of us get soapy water over our clothes.

'Kema!' I shout, giggling.

'Whoops, sorry!' Kema presses the water button and the shower starts up again.

'Okay, Firework has been very good,' Aunty Shay says. 'Sit, Firework.'

Firework sits and looks up at me. She looks like a giant soapy bubble.

'You can give her a treat now, Maz,' Aunty Shay says.

I hold out a treat on my palm.

Firework sniffs it and then her ears poke up. I nod at her and then she gently takes the treat from my hand.

Then she gobbles it up quickly

Like it's the best thing she has ever tasted.

We rinse her off and when she's squeaky clean, Aunty Shay says I can give Firework another treat.

'Sit,' I say to Firework.

Firework sits and sneezes out some of the water that's gone into her nose. ALL over me!

CHAPTER TEN

We all stand around the wooden table up on the grassy area and watch with excitement as Aunty Shay lights the candles on Anthony's cake. The cake has a really close-up photo of his face on it – it is super cool!

7
HAPPY BIRTHDAY
ANTHONY

Anthony's cheeks get red when he sees it.

'Hip, hip!' Aunty Shay shouts.

'Hooray!' we all reply.

We're so loud that Firework gets up onto her paws and looks a bit scared. I stand by Firework and scratch her head while everyone cheers, 'Hip, hip, hooray!' two more times.

When it's quiet again, Firework drops down and lays her hairy head on my feet.

'Aww,' Summer says. 'She's cute.'

Firework's tail wags slowly and her eyes start to droop.

'Who wants cake?' Anthony shouts.

We all raise our hands in the air. 'Can I please have a piece with your eyebrow on it?' I ask.

'Why would you want that?' Anthony asks.

'I've always wanted to know what an eyebrow tastes like,' I joke.

'Ewwww,' everyone says.

Anthony hands me a paper plate with his eyebrow pictured on top. Summer gets a piece with his cheek, and Mitaru gets a slice with Anthony's dark hair.

'This is delicious,' Summer says.

And she's right! We gobble up the sweet cake in no time and then have to lie on our towels to let our bellies rest.

Today has been such a fun day and one of the best birthday parties ever!

ABOUT MARY FOWLER

Mary Fowler is one of Australia's most exciting footballers and a rising global icon of the game.

She made her international debut for the Matildas when she was 15 and has performed on the world's biggest stages, including the FIFA Women's World Cup at home in Australia and the Olympics in Tokyo and Paris.

Her blend of technical brilliance, creativity, power and versatility has seen her shine for both the Matildas and Manchester City.

With her Papua New Guinean and Irish heritage shaping both her game and her outlook on life, Mary Fowler embodies a new generation of athletes redefining the sport – authentic, gifted and inspiring on and off the pitch.

Look out for more stories with

Mary Fowler!